Bob
and the
River of
Time

written and illustrated by

James Garner

Crown House Publishing Limited

www.crownhouse.co.uk

For my family and friends who
have all been so encouraging

First published by

Crown House Publishing Ltd
Crown Buildings, Bancyfelin, Carmarthen, Wales, SA33 5ND, UK
www.crownhouse.co.uk

and

Crown House Publishing Company LLC
PO Box 2223, Williston, VT 05495
www.crownhousepublishing.com

British Library Cataloguing-in-Publication Data.
A catalogue entry for this book is available from the British Library.

Print ISBN 978-1-78583-112-6
Mobi ISBN 978-1-78583-128-7
ePub ISBN 978-1-78583-129-4
ePDF ISBN 978-1-78583-130-0

LCCN 2016944970

Printed and bound in the UK by
Gomer Press, Llandysul, Ceredigion

Contents

A special thanks to my mum who, when we were toddlers, made me and my sister a book about the weather in which we took the starring role. Needless to say it was a huge part of my inspiration for this book. Her great knowledge of plant life has also been invaluable.

A Guide to Grumbledown

Bob is an ordinary fellow. He lives in Grumbledown Lodge. One day, he gets into his rowing boat and begins a topsy-turvy adventure. Throughout Bob's journey he encounters lots of wonderful plants and creatures. They are all here for you to see too, though some are harder to spot than others! See how many you can find and learn about each one at the back of the book. If you miss any, you can go back and search again!

It is
springtime
in Grumbledown. All
around there are the
sounds of birds singing chirpy
songs, fish splashing playfully in the
water and frogs croaking RIBBIT,
all in perfect harmony.

GRUMBLEDOWN LODGE

Bob climbs into his rowing boat ready
for a nice relaxing journey down the
River mumbles which flows right past his
quaint little cottage. Bob doesn't know it,
but the river holds an unusual secret and
is about to send him on a strange and
topsy-turvy adventure.

A whole spring's day passes in a flash. Before he knows it, Bob's eyes have closed and he has fallen into a deep relaxing sleep. He starts to dream about his day ... He dreams about all the amazing colours of the rainbow.

He dreams about the lambs
bouncing around in the fields
and he dreams about the
bluebells that have just come
into flower.

Time passes and Bob begins
to wake up ...

"Where am I?" thinks Bob. "I must have drifted a long way last night and what's this? The sun is high up in the sky and it's very, very hot. There isn't a cloud anywhere! The bluebells have disappeared and there are roses growing instead." All at once Bob realises, he has sailed into summer!

Mumbles Mill

This is very confusing for Bob, but being a spirited fellow he decides to carry on and enjoy the heat of the sun, the shade of the trees and the wonder of life in full flow.

A whole summer's day passes in a
flash. Before he knows it, Bob's
eyes have closed and he has
fallen into a deep relaxing
sleep. He starts to dream
about his day ...
He dreams about the
bumblebees collecting
pollen from the
flowers.

He dreams about the swallows flying high up in the sky and he dreams about the sunlight glistening on the clear water.

Time passes and Bob begins to wake up ...

"Where am I?" thinks Bob. "I must have drifted a long way last night and what's this? The leaves on the trees have changed from greens to yellows, oranges and reds. It's a bit chilly but the warm sun still peeks through the clouds now and then." All at once Bob realises, he has sailed into autumn!

This is very
confusing for Bob,
but being a spirited
fellow, he decides to carry on and
enjoy the gentle breeze which
blows the crunchy leaves off the
trees and the charming colours which
paint the whole landscape
with a warm orange glow.

A whole autumn's day passes in a flash. Before he knows it, Bob's eyes have closed and he has fallen into a deep relaxing sleep. He starts to dream about his day ...
He dreams about the cobwebs glistening with dew through the mist covered sun.

He dreams about the juicy, sweet apples growing in the orchards and he dreams about the squirrels burying acorns in the ground.

Time passes and Bob begins to wake up ...

Mumbles Church

"Where am I?" thinks Bob. "I must have drifted a long way last night and what's this? Everything has turned white and it is so cold! There are lots of red berries on the holly bushes. So many perfect little snowflakes fall from the sky, all of them shaped like tiny stars. The sun is very low in the sky and its light bounces off the snow making it very bright indeed." All at once Bob realises, he has sailed into winter!

This is very confusing for Bob, but being a spirited fellow he decides to carry on and enjoy the ... But wait! He can't go anywhere because the river has frozen over, leaving his boat stuck by the bank. Just then he notices a little log cabin in the distance, so he ties up his boat and trudges through the snow to investigate.

"Well that is lucky," thinks Bob. "It's a nice warm lodge." He pays the friendly landlady three shells for a hot meal and a bed for the night. The room is very cosy with a burning fire, and comfy clean sheets on a nice soft bed. Bob notices a poem hanging by the window which he begins to read ...

Through hazy drops of
    spring's fresh dew,
comes summer's shine
    with life all new.
Autumn falls and life
    stands still,
waiting for the winter chill.
Round and round,
    the River of Time,
on and on,
    a perfect rhyme.
Watch it all as you roam,
then life's a joy and you
    are home.

A whole winter's day
passes in a flash. Before
he knows it, Bob's eyes
have closed and he has
fallen into a deep
relaxing sleep. Only this
time he is so tired after
his walk through the cold
snow that he doesn't
dream at all, not a bit!

Time passes and Bob
begins to wake up ...

Having said thank you and farewell to the friendly landlady of the lodge, Bob walks through the now misty fields and soon arrives back at his boat. He is no stranger to the ever-changing scenery and takes it all in his stride. Just then, through the patchy mist, he notices a signpost which was covered in snow yesterday. It says "Grumbledown three miles".

Grumbledown
Three Miles

"Well that is good news," thinks Bob, as he unties the rope that holds his boat to the bank and sets off downstream. He makes extra sure to stay wide awake, which he knows will be very easy to do on such a magical misty morning.

In no time at all Bob is back home in Grumbledown. The mist has cleared revealing a wonderful spring day! "I had such a great time," he thinks. "It must be because I watched everything as I sailed along, just like it said in the poem. When it got cold and a bit scary, there was warmth and a friendly face not too far away."

"The very best thing of all is, I can do it again whenever I want because life carries on flowing and, just like the River mumbles, it flows at just the right pace so you can see all you could ever wish to see."

Thank you for keeping Bob company. He is ready to journey again whenever you want.

Cast and Crew
(in order of appearance)

In the following pages you will find information about the animals and plants Bob discovers on his journey. They are arranged in the order Bob sees them, starting in spring right through to winter. If you missed any you can always go back and look again; some you will have to look for very carefully! If you are really stuck, there are clues in the back of the book which will tell you where each character is hiding.

Bibi and Chip the Blackbirds

These two love eating worms, insects and berries. They will stay together their whole lives. See if you can spot them keeping Bob company throughout the book.

Bluebells

Simon the Centipede

Centipedes can have between 14 and 177 legs but despite the "cent" at the front of the name (from the Latin "centum", meaning 100) they never have exactly 100 legs. They are normally about 3cm long and like to eat smaller insects.

Apple blossom

Katie and the Sussex chickens

Katie loves nothing more than scratching around for big juicy worms. She lays eggs which she will sit on to keep warm, usually for about 21 days. After this a little yellow chick will hatch and CHEEP and CHIRP for one of those nice tasty worms!

Dandelion

Leon the Cinnabar Caterpillar

This hungry chap enjoys eating ragwort leaves and flowers and can grow up to 3cm long before turning into a cinnabar moth and flying away.

Tulips

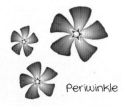

Periwinkle

Shelly the Chick

Shelly's a right little cracker, making Katie very proud indeed. Most chicks begin to replace their yellow down with normal feathers after a week or so.

Brandon the Frog

This water loving creature loves nothing more than a tasty fly which he will catch with his long sticky tongue.

Yellow flag iris

Lizzie, Bill and the ducklings: Josh, Clara and Poppy

Mallards (a type of wild duck) like to be in groups. The males have shiny green heads and the females are speckled brown. They eat small insects and fish and water plants and can be noisy when they let out their well-known QUACK QUACK!

Doug and Warren the Rabbits

They are always on the hunt for Bob's carrots, these two. You'll see lots of rabbits like Doug and Warren in the countryside. They live in holes under the ground called burrows or warrens. When they can't get at Bob's veg, they will eat grass and weeds.

Snowdrops

Radish

Lenni the Lamb and Laura the Sheep

Lenni and all her fellow lambs are born in the early spring. With boundless energy, they love bouncing around the green fields while Laura and the rest of the parents graze on the grass and keep a watchful eye out.

Gassy Gary, Whiffy William and Pungent Peter

These smelly fellows are known as stinkbugs. If they get annoyed they will release a foul odour to send the pest packing!

Daffodil

Peas

Luke the Rainbow Trout

A slippery customer, this one. He likes eating smaller fish and other water dwelling creatures, as well as flies and insects. He really enjoys being tickled too!

Kris the House Sparrow

This blighter is notoriously noisy and sociable. He is quite small and likes to eat insects, nuts and seeds.

Warts the Scarecrow

Warts is Bob's go-to guy for vegetable protection. He specialises in stopping birds from eating seeds and has sometimes been known to worry rabbits. Slugs are not part of his skill set unfortunately.

Lakey the Highland Bull

This old boy is huge, weighing in at 125 stone (which is as much as about ten people). You wouldn't want to get in his way, especially with those big horns! He eats grass and hay to keep big and strong.

Jones the Tomcat

Jones is a bit of a nomad which means he likes to wander a lot. His favourite hobbies are chasing mice and eating yummy, meaty morsels.

Abigail the Shrew

most shrews are teensy little things, growing to about 8cm long. Abigail here has tiny little eyes. She can't see very well, but she can smell all manner of things through that long quivering nose! Abigail enjoys a diet of crunchy beetles, slimy slugs and lots of other tasty insects.

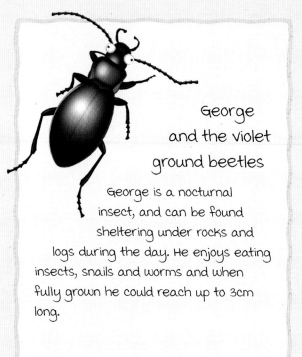

George and the violet ground beetles

George is a nocturnal insect, and can be found sheltering under rocks and logs during the day. He enjoys eating insects, snails and worms and when fully grown he could reach up to 3cm long.

Terrence the Woodcock

Terrence has a very long beak; this is very useful for catching juicy morsels. He especially likes worms and can eat more than his body weight of worms in a day. Terrence and his pals can be hard to spot, they like hiding in bogs and marshes.

Gemma the Hedgehog

If you're quiet during the evening you might see hedgehogs like Gemma scampering around looking for a bite to eat: one of their favourites is cat food! If Gemma gets scared, she will roll up into a menacing spiky ball.

Pam the Tawny Owl

Like most owls, Pam is nocturnal and very wise! She eats lots of different things including mice and other rodents. She will often swallow them whole because she gets very hungry! The bits she can't digest, she will turn into a furry, bony pellet!

Rosalind the Cabbage White Butterfly

Rosalind started life as a caterpillar, munched her way through lots of plants, went into a cocoon and emerged as a graceful butterfly.

Dandelion seeds

Kate the Coot

Kate has very big feet which help her to swim and she uses them to run across the water when taking off. She eats plants, worms and insects.

Otto the Cockerel

Also known as a rooster, Otto likes to get up early in the morning and makes sure to let everyone know about it by bellowing COCK-A-DOODLE-DOO!

Alison and the Lohmann brown chickens

Alison and her friends here lay lots of eggs; they can each lay up to 300 in one year. She is very friendly and inquisitive.

Alfie the Crested Grebe

This spiky individual can mostly be found living on lakes and slow flowing rivers. He mainly eats fish but will also eat frogs and insects.

weeping willow leaves

Alastair the Emperor Dragonfly

This colourful creature can grow up to 8cm long. He likes eating butterflies and tadpoles but doesn't live for very long, normally just two or three weeks.

Rose

Horse chestnut leaf

Fudge the Blowfly

Fudge isn't a fussy eater, she will quite happily tuck into a smelly, rotten piece of meat. She also lays her eggs on anything meaty so that when her baby maggots hatch they have a delicious meal waiting for them.

Jasper and the honeybees

Jasper is always on the go collecting nectar from flowers. He takes the nectar back to his hive and it is turned into a delicious sweet honey which he and the rest of his colony will live on.

Ringo the minotaur Beetle

This mighty fellow feeds on dung! minotaur beetles lay their eggs in tunnels and drag dung back to their nests to feed their young. They grow up to be around 2cm long.

Vanessa the Grasshopper

Vanessa here enjoys eating grasses and leaves as well as the farmer's crops. She can jump 20 times her own body length, which is like a human jumping the entire length of a basketball court and a little bit more! In the evening you can sometimes hear grasshoppers rubbing their back legs against their wings.

Otis and the greenflies

Poor Otis is actually a bit of a pest. Otis and his mates get onto Bob's plants and don't do them any good at all by sucking the sap out of them. To make things worse, their saliva is toxic to the plants.

Sunflower

Strawberries

Agnes and the goats

Agnes loves eating grass, weeds, flowers, small trees, bushes – pretty much anything that grows and some things that don't! Her offspring are called kids.

Grapes

Ian the Kingfisher

This colourful chap knows how to fish! He'll sit on a perch near the water, spy his target and sweep in for the prize in a flash.

Leah and Sam the Ladybirds

These spotty guys are small beetles, normally around 1cm long. Bob is always happy to see them in his garden as they eat all the pests that munch his flowers.

Pansies

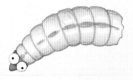

Tomatoes

Dave the mole

Dave gets his kicks by making a mess of the lawn with lots of little piles of soil. His big hands help him to burrow lots of tunnels where he can trap his favourite dinner – worms!

Micky and the maggots

Micky is a bit of a smelly fella, that's because he loves being around anything rotten! He is widely considered to be a pest, but not by fishermen. Trouble is, micky here is a slippery customer and is very good at wriggling off the hook. micky will be a maggot for around four to ten days, then he will turn into a fly and buzz off!

Murphy the Sheepdog

This handsome fellow is a border collie. He is extremely intelligent and will always do what he is told; this makes him very good at rounding up sheep for the farmer.

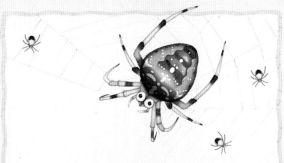

Gill and the garden spiders

Commonly known as garden spiders, these guys hatch in the spring and grow nice and big in the summer until they are fully grown in the autumn. They are more noticeable in autumn. You can see them perched on their webs, which they attach to all sorts of things. It normally takes about one hour to build a web. Their webs are very sticky and hard to see, making them great traps for flies.

Bean and the swallows

Bean won't stand for the cold, she'll only show her face when the weather is warm and is so fussy about this that she'll fly all the way to Africa to prove her point. She is very good at finding her way home and will go to the same place in the UK to nest every year.

Barb and the wasps

Anything sweet and Barb will be buzzing around it like a shot, especially jam! You will see lots of wasps when there is fruit growing. They have a nasty sting which they will use if they feel threatened.

milk thistle

Cherries

Jim, Jim, Jim, Bex and Jim the Ants

These chaps are tough, lifting up to 50 times their own body weight! That's like a human picking up a hippo! They live in a nest with about 5,000 other ants.

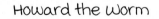

Howard the Worm

Howard the worm is often wriggling and squiggling. He lives in the earth and loves eating rotten leaves and soil. Yum!

Clematis

Denzel the Bumblebee

Denzel is a sociable guy and lives in a colony ruled by a queen bee. He will sting if he needs to but is generally too chilled out to bother, preferring to get on with his job of collecting pollen from flowers and feasting on nectar.

Stinging nettle

Harry the Devil's Coach Horse Beetle

Harry can give quite a nip with those pincers and is about 3cm long. Much like those smelly stinkbugs, Harry can give off a smelly stench if he is threatened. He is nocturnal and loves eating insects, spiders and slugs.

Raspberries

Michael the Fox

Michael is shrewd and sneaky, often trying to work out how to get at the farmer's chickens. He prefers to be active at night and will sleep during the day unless he is really hungry.

Honor and the glow-worms

What vibrant little things! Only the females glow this wonderful bright yellow green colour. Honor and her friends come out at night in early summer. Their young like to eat snails and slugs!

Oak leaf

Tash and the midges

These tiny things are barely noticeable but are a bit of a nuisance as they like biting people. Worse still, the bites can get really itchy and make you look spotty! You will often see midges in groups near water, especially in the early evening.

Sue the moth

If you leave your window open and the lights on, Sue will be in like a shot! She drinks nectar from flowers or sap from trees.

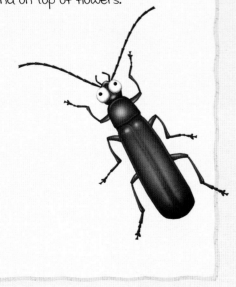

John and the soldier beetles

John and his mates can be found all over the place. Soldier beetles grow up to 1cm long and feed on pollen, nectar and sometimes small insects, which they find on top of flowers.

Derek the Barn Owl

Mice and other rodents are Derek's favourite snack. He is nocturnal but sometimes he hunts for food in the daytime. He is recognisable by his ear piercing screech which you might be lucky enough to hear during the evening.

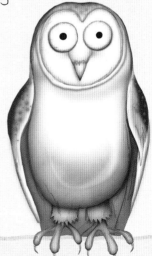

Stevie and the donkeys

Donkeys are very much like horses only they are smaller, have bigger ears and instead of neighing they bellow out a HEE-HAW noise which we call braying. They graze on grass and are known to be rather stubborn.

Leigh the Woodpecker

This excitable chap is never far from a tree. His favourite foods are insects and grubs but he will also eat fruit and nuts. Woodpeckers make neat little holes in the trunks of trees where they build their nests and bring up their baby woodpeckers.

James the Heron

James has a very long neck and skinny legs; overall he is about one metre tall. He enjoys catching fish almost as much as eating them. For such a large creature, he is surprisingly difficult to spot.

Bulrush

Oscar the Collared Dove

Oscar and his chums like to eat seeds and grains. When Oscar walks, his head bobs backwards and forwards making him look like he's headbanging.

Chrysanthemum

Flash and Parsley the Snails

These two slimy chaps are very, very slow. They will take a whole hour to travel one metre! They eat most plants easily as they have thousands of tiny teeth on their tongues (known as a radula)!

Fly agaric mushroom (poisonous)

Hamish the Pig

As you can see, Hamish has a big nose. This is used to sniff out food in the ground. He is an omnivore which means he will eat both meat and vegetables. He'll eat just about anything really!

Turnip

Joleen the Squirrel

Acorn

Joleen is a red squirrel. She has a very big, bushy tail — it's nearly the same size as the rest of her. This is probably to help her keep her balance when scampering through trees. She mainly eats seeds and nuts including hazelnuts, chestnuts and acorns.

Apples

Freddy and Rob the Toads

These warty skinned fellows grow up to 8cm. Female toads can grow up to 13cm! They are hungry chaps and eat lots of creepy crawlies like worms, beetles, flies and slugs which they swallow whole, gulp after gulp!

Andy and the woodlice

Andy and his friends can usually be found in dark and damp places. They are mostly nocturnal but do venture out in the day sometimes. Andy's favourite food is rotting plants!

Horse mushroom

Emily the Horsefly

Watch out for this one! Emily is silent on her approach, but if she lands on you she will give you a nip which will itch for days! You'll find her where there are lots of horses or cows when it's warm.

Lords-and-ladies
(poisonous)

Pat and the cows

While we have one chamber in our stomachs to digest food, Pat and her friends each have four! They will regurgitate partly digested food and chew on it some more – yum, yum! This is called "chewing the cud". Pat's young get their milk from the big pink udder swinging from her belly. To communicate, Pat makes a very distinctive MOOOOO.

Richard the Dormouse

Richard here likes sleeping – a lot. He eats loads of nuts and berries during the autumn. As soon as the weather gets chilly, he will hibernate for the winter. Occasionally, he might wake up during this long sleep, have a quick nibble and then go back to bed!

Fern

Hazelnut

Ethan and the earwigs

Ethan and friends like hiding under rocks and prefer venturing out at night. They eat smaller insects as well as some plants. They grow to just over 2cm long. The pincers at the back are for defence and can give a nasty nip!

Pampas grass

Tanya the Crane Fly

Sometimes called daddy-long-legs, crane flies like Tanya can grow up to 7cm but most of that size is those long legs! Their bodies only grow to about 3cm long. Crane flies don't eat very much; their job is to lay eggs which turn into larvae, called leatherjackets because of their tough brown skin. These eventually turn into crane flies and round and round it goes!

Pear

Paul the Graveyard Cat

This is the vicar's cat. He is a scatty creature and loves chasing after the mice and other rodents in the graveyard.

Oliver and the ravens

Oliver is a raven. Ravens are closely related to crows. They are big birds, around 70cm long and their wingspan can be well over a metre! They like to eat just about anything from insects and seeds to rodents and young birds!

Pumpkin

Rowan the Brown Rat

Rowan's a bit of a greedy guts and will munch his way through almost anything. He's a big old boy, his breed sometimes grow as long as half a metre (tail included)! He has a very good sense of hearing so he'll always know you're coming!

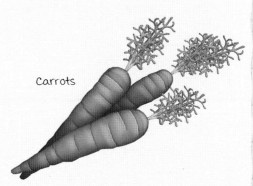

Carrots

Samantha the House Spider

Samantha here has eight long legs and this makes her very quick. She sits in a fine web waiting for insects to wander past and then she pounces!

Parsnips

Ben the Great Crested Newt

If you want to see Ben and his mates, you will need to go to a pond or a bog. They are happy both on land and in the water. Newts eat insects, water snails and tadpoles. They might grow up to 18cm long.

Potatoes

Sssebastian the Sssnake

Sebastian is a wriggly adder and is about 60cm long. He loves nothing more than munching on rodents like small mice and shrews. Adders have a venomous bite but rarely use it on humans; unless they feel threatened, they prefer to slither off and hide.

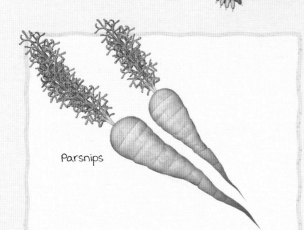

Jane, Dan, Brad, Tim, Tom, Hilary and Sarah the Red Velvet mites

Also known as rain bugs, these little guys look just like tiny red spiders. They are parasites, sucking the blood of insects and spiders. They grow to be around 5mm long.

Honesty

Ana the Badger

Blackberry

Ana and her family live underground in setts. She is faster than she looks and can run at nearly 20 miles per hour! She is not a fussy eater and will happily tuck into insects, worms, birds and small mammals as well as nuts and fruit.

Claudia the Bat

Claudia is a great fan of just hanging around! Bats are quite small, not getting any bigger than about 5cm, but their wingspans can reach up to 25cm. Bats don't see very well and use a combination of their eyes and sounds which echo when flying. They hunt at night enjoying delicious insects.

Onion

Heather and the robins

Chinese lantern

Robins like Heather can be quite tame especially during the winter. She will hang around hoping to be fed some breadcrumbs. Like most birds, she enjoys eating insects, worms and seeds. Robins like their space and if other robins get in their way, they can become quite angry!

Holly

Brussels Sprout

mistletoe

Tony the Turkey

Tony may not exactly be an oil painting, but what he lacks in looks, he makes up for in personality. He'll eat a variety of food including seeds, greens and insects. He is known for his unusual GOBBLE GOBBLE noise!

Finn the Horse

Finn is a big horse whose main hobby is eating grass. His other hobby is sleeping which he can do standing up. Finn really does live the life!

Winter jasmine

Gordon the Goose

Geese can be noisy creatures and Gordon is no exception, some people have them instead of guard dogs! Gordon likes to eat plants, grains and grasses.

Walnut

Chestnut

Yew leaves (poisonous)

Puddles the Snowman

Created by the kids of Grumbledown, Puddles can take on a lot of different shapes and will go on as many different adventures as the kids' imaginations can come up with (which is a lot!). Try building a snowman yourself next time it's snowing.

Stuart the Blue Tit

If you put nuts out in the garden, this brightly coloured guy will be one of the first to start pecking at them. He will be more than happy eating spiders and insects too.

Pine tree

Jersey cream clematis

Amber the Otter

Otters like Amber here love fish, which is what they eat most of the time, but for a snack they might enjoy the odd frog or crayfish. They are great swimmers but are also very hard to spot.

Lucas the Buck and Flo the Doe

As you may have guessed, a buck is a male deer and a doe is a female deer. They can be found in the countryside where they eat most plants.

Pine cone

Poppy

Anthony the Slug

This slippery, slimy chap is very much like a snail only without the mobile home. Watch out for him in your lettuce sandwich!

Winter aconite

Lily of the valley

Willow the Water Vole

Willow is a great swimmer and she is quite hard to spot. Including their tails, the bigger water voles can reach up to 30cm long. They live in burrows which they make in river banks and eat grass, plants and sometimes fruit.

Mary the Swan

She may appear graceful and calm, but underneath the water those legs are paddling away. Swans prefer to eat greens like pondweed but they will sometimes eat the odd insect or tadpole!

Crocus

Reg and the fleas

Reg is a real pain, and so are his mates. He is known as a parasite which means he uses other creatures as his home. What's worse, he will drink his host's blood making lots of itchy bites. He can jump 200 times his own height which is like an adult human jumping the height of the Empire State Building in New York!

Snake's head fritillary

Phelix the Pheasant

Pheasants are omnivores; they like to eat insects, worms, plants and seeds. They make their nests on the ground and can often be heard making their CHIRP CHIRP sound all over the countryside.

Elderflower

Ivy

Jenny the Angle Shades Caterpillar

Like her close relation the cinnabar caterpillar, Jenny will eat her way through loads of plants before going into her cocoon and turning into an angle shades moth.

Grace the Moorhen and Alex the Worm

moorhens are like coots but they are a bit smaller, more secretive and have yellow and red beaks instead of white. They both like a tasty worm though, which is unfortunate for Alex here.

Spring onion

Zoe the millipede

Zoe has over 150 legs; this means Zoe needs lots of shoes ... Some species of millipede can grow up to 28cm long, but Zoe is only about 6cm. Like the stinkbugs, they can release a smelly liquid if they feel threatened.

Isobel the Peacock Butterfly

Isobel is a very colourful butterfly. Her markings look like extra eyes — she uses them to scare off other creatures like birds which think she might make a tasty snack! She is about 6cm from wing to wing and, like most butterflies, she drinks nectar from flowers.

Nic the Cat and Scooter the Dog

Bob's favourite furry companions, both offering unconditional love. Scooter is likely to get under Bob's feet while Nic is happy off adventuring on her own but always comes back to sit on Bob's lap.

Bob!

Where Are They Hiding?

Did you find them all? Here are clues to where all those plants
and critters are hiding, in case you're really stuck!

28

14

27

14

26

25

8

12

22

15

24

23 21

20

19 18 17

2

Clues for pages 4–5

Mumbles Mill

Clues for pages 10-11

56

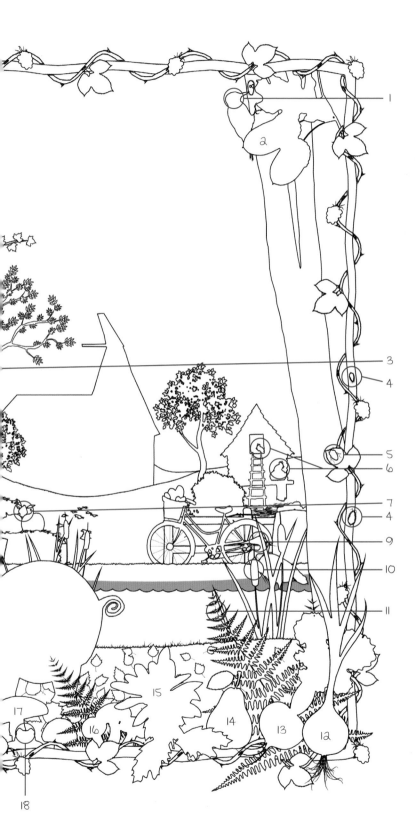

Clues for pages 12–13

Clues for pages 14–15

Clues for pages 16–17

1 Yew leaves (poisonous) 42

2 Holly 42

3 Walnut 42

4 Hazelnut 38

5 mistletoe 42

6 Chestnut 42

7 Lucas the Buck 43

8 Kris the House Sparrow 26

9 Chip the Blackbird 24

10 Bibi the Blackbird 24

11 Pine cone 43

Grumbledown
Three Miles

THE NED